This book belongs to:

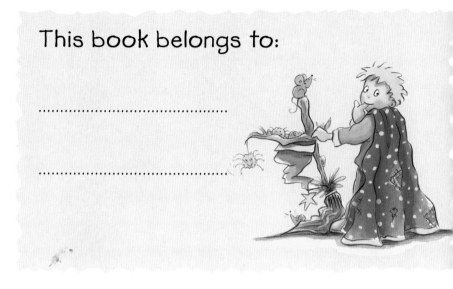

....

....

Written by Kath Smith
Illustrated by Caroline Jayne Church
Designed by Andrea Newton
Language consultant: Betty Root

This is a Parragon Publishing book
This edition published in 2005

Parragon Publishing
Queen Street House
4 Queen Street
Bath BA1 1HE, UK

Copyright © Parragon 2002
Printed in China.

ISBN 1-40541-891-5

The Little Friends
Wizards are Magic

p

Scruffy Wizard Buffy

Buffy was a wizard who
Was always good and kind.
So others always turned to him—
They knew he wouldn't mind.

If someone needed magic,
Or something warm to wear,
They went to see their kindly friend.
He always seemed to care.

But though he was kind-hearted,
And NEVER cross or huffy,
Buffy had a little fault—
He always looked so scruffy!

His cloak was old and full of holes—
A beggar had his best.
He never wore his wizard's hat—
It was a spider's nest!

As for Buffy's broomstick—
It was a mouse retreat.
So while the other wizards flew,
Poor Buffy used his feet.

But Buffy never did complain.
He'd always smile and say,
"Take it, with *my* blessing ..."
Then he'd give his things away.

One day Fairy Lily came
To pick up a special spell.
"He looks so shabby," Lily thought,
"He needs OUR help as well."

Off she flew to see her friends,
"He's such a dreadful sight!
His clothes are in such tatters.
It really is not right!"

When the others looked at him,
They realized it was true.
"Let's put our heads together,
To see what we can do!"

The princesses gave some jewelry—
The finest they could find.
The fairies gave some sparkle dust—
The magic, glowing kind.

The knights gave richest fabric—
Nothing but the best!
The wizards cast a secret spell,
And magic did the rest.

They conjured up a splendid cloak,
A gift for kind old Buffy.
Delighted, Buffy laughed and cried,
"Goodbye to Mr. Scruffy!"

Whizzy Wizard Izzy

Izzy, the whizzy wizard,
Loved to race around.
Often he would move so fast,
He'd barely touch the ground.

Before he finished one thing,
He'd move on to the next,
I'm sure you can imagine,
This left some people vexed!

In fact, he was so speedy,
The other wizards said,
The only time he ever stopped
Was when he went to bed.

Because he was so frantic,
His spells would rarely work.
When he twirled his wand around,
Things often went beserk.

A magic sleeping potion,
Could turn to mushroom stew.
And when he asked his broom to fly,
It knew not what to do!

Whenever someone came to lunch
And asked for tea or coffee,
They'd end up drinking something else,
Like mud, or chewy toffee!

He even turned poor Heather
Into a tiny elf.
He went about his business—
SHE wasn't quite herself!

Then Heather said in anger,
"This time I've had enough.
Something really must be done
To stop this silly stuff."

So Heather, who was very smart,
Thought hard and gave a frown,
Then she cried, "I've got the answer!
He has to slow right down."

Izzy's problem was, you see,
He didn't stop to think.
But Heather put an end to that
With a bubbling magic drink.

Now when Izzy casts a spell,
He has to STOP and sneeze.
This gives him time to see if it's right,
then cast his spell with ease.

Grumpy Wizard Dumpy

Far away in Wizard Wood
Lived grumbling Wizard Dumpy.
He never seemed to laugh or smile.
His face was always grumpy.

When someone said, "Good morning!"
He'd mutter, "What's so good?"
And when they shouted, "Hi, there!"
He'd ignore them if he could.

23

Dumpy was so surly,
He never joined in the fun.
He was, of all the wizards there,
The only grumpy one.

"A wizard shouldn't be so sad,"
Decided Princess Polly.
"He needs someone to cheer him up,
And make him much more jolly."

So Polly asked him riddles,
And told jokes that made her roar.
But Dumpy only sighed and said,
"What are you laughing for?"

Then early one fine morning,
She knocked on Dumpy's door.
But Dumpy did not answer,
And then she heard a snore.

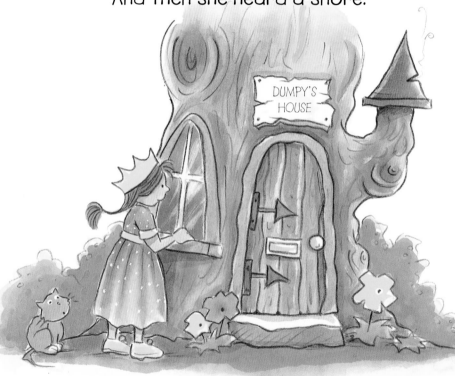

She looked in through the window
As Dumpy left his bed.
Poor Dumpy didn't rise and shine,
But tumbled out instead.

Since Dumpy's bed was floating,
The fall was pretty bad.
If Dumpy fell like that each day,
No wonder he was sad!

Polly visited Fairy Heather,
Who thought a bit, then said,
"I think that something must be done,
To help him out of bed!"

So Heather waved her magic wand
In front of Dumpy's face.
Then, in a cloud of magic dust,
Appeared a long staircase.

Now Dumpy starts his mornings
The way a wizard should—
By walking down a staircase ...
And in a mood that's good!